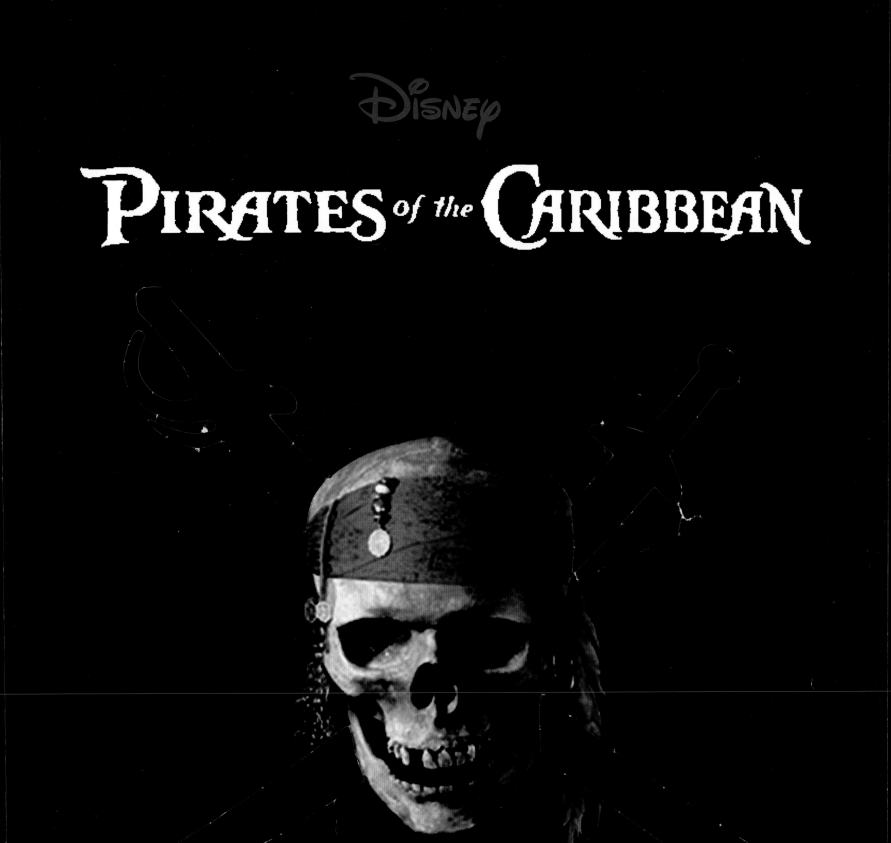

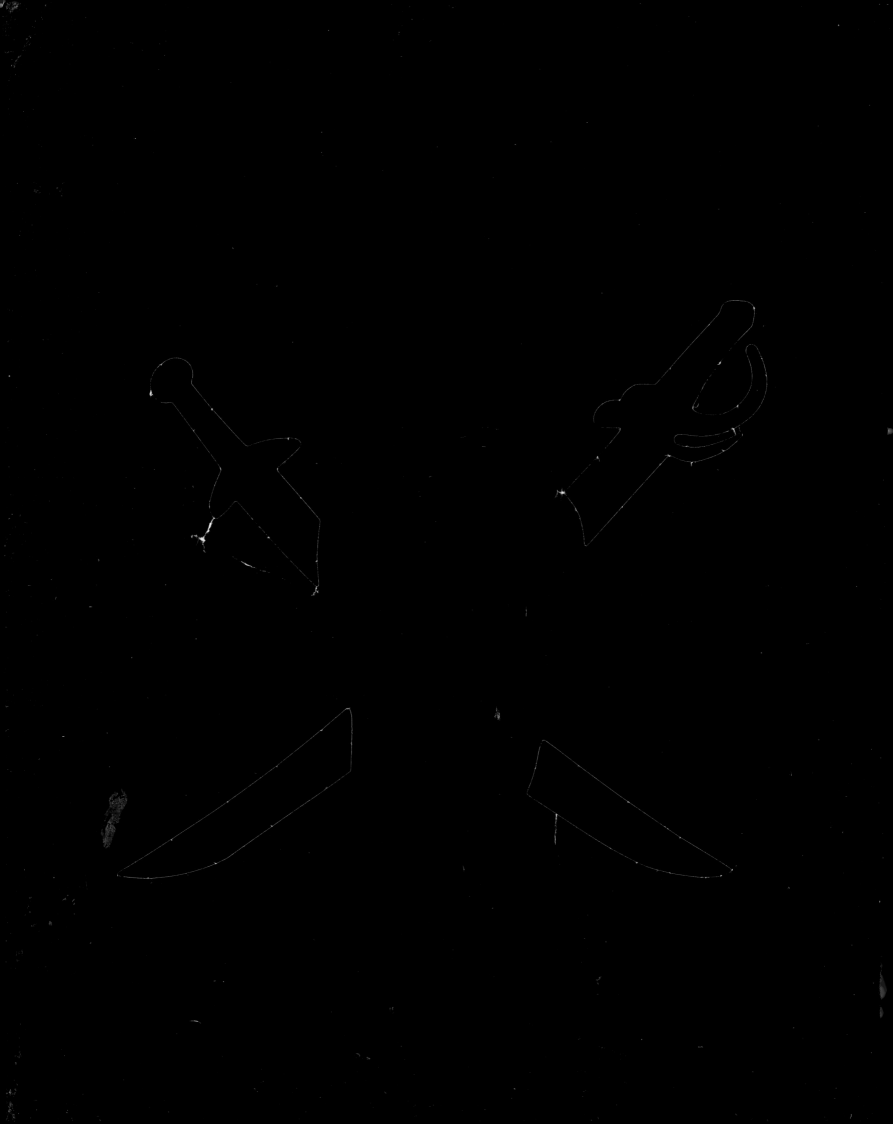

Disney
PIRATES of the CARIBBEA

THE VISUAL GUIDE

BY RICHARD PLATT

Contents

Foreword
by Jerry Bruckheimer

I was young, in love with movies, and my eyes were glued to the screen, mesmerized, watching the daring, exciting, funny and acrobatic exploits of The Crimson Pirate, played by the great Burt Lancaster. Freewheeling, rebellious, unafraid to defy authority at every turn, the wind at your back and your ship pointed directly toward the freedom of the seven seas...what could be more fun than being a pirate...or at least being a pirate in the movies? I certainly had my favorite pirate films as a kid, including *Captain Blood*, *The Black Pirate*, and *Treasure Island*, all of them classics of swashbuckling and skullduggery.

And then, suddenly, as the world moved toward a new century, pirate movies went away. Vanished. Nobody cared any more, the skull and crossbones disappeared from the big screen. In a world of high-speed and hip-hop, the adventures of 18th century buccaneers had lost their relevancy...or had they?

Because at Disneyland in Anaheim, California, as well as other Disney parks around the world, the mid-1960s attraction known as "Pirates of the Caribbean" had been drawing throngs since its opening, first as a miraculous leap of technology, and then as a nostalgic ride through the memories of grownups, and the imagination of their children. And when Walt Disney Studios asked me to find a way to translate the fun ride into a two-hour-plus feature film extravaganza, nothing could have excited me more. My dream of making a motion picture about pirates was about to come true. And the popularity of the movie that finally emerged in 2003, *Pirates of the Caribbean: The Curse of the Black Pearl*, not only fulfilled my hopes, but exceeded them. And thankfully, audiences around the world seemed to agree that we had not only breathed new life into a dead genre, but had actually reinvented it.

We wanted to take the pirate genre to a new level, one that had all the thrills and romance that you would expect from a big adventure, but with original, unforgettable characters, state-of-the-art visual effects and a tip of the hat to the original Disneyland attraction, while taking off in whole new directions. Our director, Gore Verbinski, has a wonderful sense of humor and great storytelling skills. His enthusiasm is like a little kid's. He loves to work with actors, and actors love him. He was the perfect director for the project. As writers, we brought in the team of Ted Elliott and Terry Rossio—two wonderful writers who created a big hit with *Shrek*—to put our stamp on a draft by Jay Wolpert and Stuart Beattie which Disney first handed over to us. Ted and Terry brought in the element of the supernatural laced with lots of humor, which gave the story an edge that really interested me.

Then we had our stars, and it soon became clear after the film was released that Johnny Depp had created a brand-new, authentic motion picture icon with his performance as Captain Jack Sparrow. Johnny's known for creating his own characters, and he had a definite vision for Jack Sparrow which was completely unique. We just let him go and he came up with this off-center, yet very shrewd pirate, with his dreadlocks, gold teeth and grand assortment of ornamental beads and charms. He can't quite hold his balance, his speech is a bit slurred, so you assume he's either drunk, seasick or he's been on a ship too long. But it's all an act perpetrated for effect. And strange as it seems, it's also part of Captain Jack's charm. The Academy of Motion Picture Arts and Sciences certainly thought so, honoring Johnny with an Oscar nomination for Best Actor. We cast Orlando Bloom as Will Turner after he appeared in another of my productions, *Black Hawk Down*. I knew Orlando's time would come. I just didn't know how lucky we'd be to grab him before all the frenzy started with the *Lord of the Rings* films. We considered many young actresses for the role of Elizabeth Swann, but beauty alone was not enough. With Keira Knightley, who was then 17-years-old, we found beauty, brains, and boldness, a great combination.

Millions of people from 8 to 80 took the ride with us, and clearly, they wanted more. So now we've created *Pirates of the Caribbean: Dead Man's Chest*, which will be followed by a third film as well, reuniting nearly the whole gang from the first film, with several exciting new additions as well. Gore is back, as are Ted and Terry, and of course Johnny, Orlando, Keira and much of the supporting cast. But we weren't interested in just doing a re-tread. Instead, everything in the first film gets pushed forward in *Dead Man's Chest*, and will be pushed even further in the third Pirates movie. We love these characters and want to see what happens with them, deepening the characterizations and continuing the story. Much of the backdrop of *Dead Man's Chest* is based on pirate lore, and the mythology of the seven seas, using elements of 18th century British history as a springboard. We have an astonishing new villain with Davy Jones, who along with his crew is unlike anything that's been seen before, as well as the power-mad English aristocrat Lord Cutler Beckett of the East India Trading Company.

Our new production designer, an amazing creative individual named Rick Heinrichs, has added so many wonderful nuances to *Dead Man's Chest*, including epic-sized sets, a re-designed and re-built *Black Pearl*, and the *Flying Dutchman*, Davy Jones' fantastic mystery ship. And we've filmed, appropriate to our film's title, in some of the most exotic locations in all the Caribbean, including the rugged tropical paradise islands of Dominica and St. Vincent, and on the islands and turquoise oceans of the Bahamas.

This new DK book is a wonderful entry into the world of *Pirates of the Caribbean: The Curse of the Black Pearl* and *Pirates of the Caribbean: Dead Man's Chest*, filled with pictures, illustrations and loaded with information about both films. Like the original Disneyland "Pirates of the Caribbean," we've tried to make our movies an "E" ticket attraction which everyone can ride together. So step aboard, mates, and sail off with us once again under the flag of adventure and imagination as limitless as the sea that stretches all the way to the far horizon. Keelhauling and walking the plank are definitely forbidden on this voyage!

Jerry Bruckheimer

Introduction

Captain Jack Sparrow is a pirate without a ship. Robbed of it by a mutinous crew, he wants it back. Nothing will stop him—not even the British Navy or cursed Aztec Gold. But Jack's quest turns out to be more difficult than he imagined when a rebellious governor's daughter and a plucky blacksmith get in the way. Recovering the *Black Pearl* isn't the end of Jack's adventures in the Caribbean. Just as he thinks he is safe, a ghostly comrade appears to remind him of a bargain he made thirteen years ago. Then his only hope of saving himself lies in finding a mysterious chest—and the beating heart within it.

Caribbean

ISLANDS OF THE CARIBBEAN

Atlantic Ocean

Sea

Jack Sparrow

Born on a pirate ship in a typhoon, Captain Jack Sparrow has seawater in his veins. At least, that's what his friends say. His enemies don't care whether his heart pumps blood, water, or rum. They just want to see him at the end of a hangman's rope, or at the bottom of the sea. But Jack has an uncanny knack for escaping their clutches. Through bravery, luck, and cunning, he manages to slip out of the tightest fixes.

The beads and trinkets in Jack's hair have been gathered from all over the world. Each one reminds him of a different adventure

Hard to Starboard!

Jack is happiest at the helm of the *Black Pearl*. For him it is much more than "a keel; a hull; a deck and sails..." —it's freedom. Though his crew mutinied, he will always be Captain Jack Sparrow, and the *Pearl* will always be his.

TATTOOED AND BRANDED
Below the blue tattoo of a sparrow on Jack's right arm is a faint "P"—proof that he has been accused of piracy and was branded with a red-hot iron.

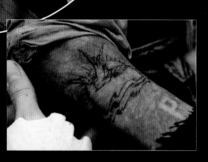

Hard-wearing linen pants

Elizabeth's Choker

Jack seems like a desperate pirate who lets nothing stand between him and freedom or treasure. But he's not all bad. His threat to choke Elizabeth with the manacles that bind his hands is a bluff. After all, how could he kill a pretty woman whom he has just saved from a watery grave?

Dressed to Kill

There's a touch of the dandy about Jack, and his outfit shows off his status as captain. Long pants, sea boots, and knotted sash set him apart from his motley crew.

A Hit with the Ladies!

Jack's wit, charm, and generous spirit make him popular company. So popular, in fact, that he has trouble remembering names and faces. The ladies in the taverns of Tortuga haven't forgotten Jack though, and they all think a slap or two will improve his memory.

Bottle stands upright on a pitching ship

Yo Ho Ho and a Bottle of Rum
Drinking is one of the most popular of pirate pleasures. Like all pirates, Jack believes that "rum gets you through times of no money better than money gets you through times of no rum."

When there's trouble on board, Jack's sword is rarely in its scabbard

King of Thieves

Jack loves gold. On *Isla de Muerta* he drapes himself with treasure. With pearls around his neck and rings on his fingers, a finishing touch is a jewel-encrusted gold crown.

Sneaky Jack

Captain Jack's silver tongue helps him to weasel his way past the most alert sentries—at least for a while. To get on board the *Interceptor*, he tells its guards that the *Black Pearl* can outsail any other ship. While they argue about whether or not the *Pearl* and its crew of cursed sailors even exists, Jack slips onto the deck.

No Escape?

When fine words don't work, trickery usually does. Surrounded by bayonets and almost certainly bound for the gallows, Jack takes Elizabeth hostage. A handy crane hoists him quickly out of harm's way, and he slides down a rope to make good his escape.

11

Pirate Possessions

Jack has few worldly goods to his name—they are all too easily stolen, gambled away, or lost overboard—but what he does have he holds dear. His grandest possession is his ship, the *Black Pearl*, while smaller items, like his hat, have sentimental value. Weapons are the tools of a pirate's trade, so Jack never likes to lend or borrow them. An unusual compass is the most special of all his things. He consults it constantly and is wary about giving his most trusted shipmates even a glance at its gently spinning dial.

Lid shows map of the heavens

Central shadow vane makes compass work as a sundial

Compass disk sliced from a walrus tusk

Magnetic Marvel

Although it appears to be useless (the needle never points to the north,) Jack's compass has supernatural qualities. The compass cannot be used to navigate in a conventional sense, but it does direct the owner to whatever he or she most desires. Jack acquired the compass from a voodoo priestess named Tia Dalma seven years earlier.

Domed cover made from pure lapis lazuli

Bone Paddle

Nobody escapes from a Turkish prison alive, so Jack sneaks inside a coffin to get out. The guards drop the dead prisoners from a clifftop and the falling tide carries the caskets out to sea. Something stirs within one of the bobbing boxes. Jack Sparrow pops up and borrows a handy oar from his fellow passenger.

Rounded hip joint makes a comfortable handhold

Foot doubles as oar blade

PULLING YOUR LEG

"Sorry mate," quips Jack as he wrenches a bony oar from a rotting hip. It lasts just long enough to paddle him as far as the *Black Pearl*. "If you ask right, there's always someone willing to give you a leg-up," he tells Gibbs.

Fighting Jack

Jack has become an expert buccaneer, defending himself with his trusty sword and pistol. An Italian fencing master taught him many of his sword skills—in exchange for a captured cargo of Chinese silk. Marksmanship took him a little longer to master. He trained himself to shoot by taking aim at empty wine bottles tossed from the *Pearl*'s deck rail. A bucket of shot and a sack of gunpowder later, he could hit nine out of ten bottles.

COLD STEEL

Jack's saber is longer than the cutlass that most pirates favor. For a pirate who's in trouble as much as Jack, it's important to keep his enemies a couple of extra inches away. Jack's battle with Barbossa on *Isla de Muerta* proves he made a sensible choice as he more than matches his archenemy blow for blow.

Handguard stops blood from running down the blade

Jack keeps the cutting edge extremely sharp

Decorative design inlaid in silver

Flint springs forward when the trigger is pulled, striking sparks to ignite gunpowder

HOT POWDER

Jack cherishes his flintlock pistol, but he never pulls the trigger. He vowed not to fire the gun except in a fair fight with Barbossa. When Jack's treacherous first mate marooned him on a desert island, he gave Jack his pistol and just one shot—to kill himself. But Jack escaped, and nine years later he gets his revenge, shooting Barbossa on *Isla de Muerta*.

Jack cleans and polishes the barrel daily to clean off the rust that forms quickly in the salty sea air

Thanks to its heavy pommel, gun doubles as a lethal club

Essential Hat

Any self-respecting pirate captain feels naked without his hat. Jack Sparrow is no exception. The black tricorn is battered and faded, but still serves him well. It's practical as well as decorative: he's filled it with cool fresh water to drink at wells and trapped deadly scorpions in its domed crown.

Faded leather has been scorched by Caribbean sun and beaten by harsh sea winds

Port Royal

Founded by the English, Port Royal is a bustling harbor town situated on the eastern tip of Jamaica. The town is built around Fort Charles, England's biggest government fort in the Caribbean. Or at least it was. A battering from the cannons of the *Black Pearl* leaves the fort quite a lot smaller—and boosts the pirates' power.

Docks and Castle

Towering over the town, Fort Charles is supposed to protect the ships of the Royal Navy moored in the harbor below. The cannons that point out from the battlements are a menacing warning to pirates cruising offshore. However, the fort's garrison is helpless when Jack and Will sneak on board the *Dauntless* and sail it out to sea.

HARBORMASTER ON THE MAKE

With his wig, spectacles, and tricorn hat, the Harbormaster seems like a loyal servant of the king, but not everything is as it seems. Years of mixing with maritime riffraff have corrupted him. When Jack offers a small bribe to keep his arrival secret, the Harbormaster cannot resist.

Bribes help the Harbormaster to buy fine clothes he could not afford on his meager government salary

LIAR'S LOG

The Harbormaster's ledger records the details of every ship and sailor tying up at the dock. Jack's handful of coins ensures that he doesn't appear in it.

GONE FISHING

It's not all business at Port Royal's wharf. There's always time to fit in a bit of angling. This ragged lad hopes to catch enough for dinner by the time the sun goes down.

Shopping Spree

Stretching back from the harbor, shops jostle for space with Port Royal's many taverns. Here an enterprising captain can find everything he needs, from tar for a ship's bottom to smuggled lace for his lady love.

The Bit 'n' Stirrup supplies bits, bridles, and lots of other equipment for Port Royal's horses, including those from Fort Charles.

As well as regular remedies, the apothecary mixes potions to mend a broken heart or to stop a dog from straying. When merchant ships dock, he's kept busy selling pox cures to the crew.

With all the vessels dropping anchor at Port Royal there is a constant supply of sailors looking for a hearty meal and a bed for the night. Not all innkeepers welcome pirates but at the Whale and Waterspout, old Mr Garrett turns a blind eye—as long as his guests pay their bill in full.

Sweet Fruit and Sewers

Though Port Royal's street markets overflow with juicy tropical fruit, the air is far from sweet. The town doubled in size in 10 years, and the sewer system can't cope.

CONTRABAND CARGOES

Port Royal's customs officials are just as corrupt as the Harbormaster. In exchange for a share of a ship's cargo, they turn their backs while smugglers land their goods—free of import duty. Then the smugglers load up with rum and sugar to smuggle back to America.

THAT SINKING FEELING

Captain Jack Sparrow makes an unusual yet graceful entrance to Port Royal harbor. He steps onto the wooden dock from the masthead of the purloined fishing trawler, the *Jolly Mon.* Jack makes port just in time—despite bailing as fast as he can, his craft sinks silently beneath him.

15

Governor Swann

Appointed by the King of England, Wetherby Swann is the proud Governor of the British colony at Port Royal on the vibrant and prosperous island of Jamaica. Undoubtedly Swann is charming and polite but it's no secret that he hasn't the skill to govern his rebellious daughter Elizabeth, let alone an entire island!

Though his wig makes his head hot and itchy, Swann feels undressed without it

Loving Father

Since the death of his wife, Governor Swann has raised his daughter Elizabeth on his own. Over the years Elizabeth has blossomed into a beautiful young lady, although at times she drives her father to distraction with her willfulness and disregard for propriety!

LIVING LIKE A LORD

Set in the fashionable St. Paul's district, Governor Swann's grand mansion is far from the squalor of Port Royal's docks and slums.

Luxurious ostrich feathers trim his tricorn hat

Aristocratic Attire

Ruling over a British colony demands a certain authority, and Governor Swann dresses to impress. His fashionable frock coat comes from his London tailor, and his cravat from Paris. It's a shame he does not pay as much attention to his work as he does to his appearance.

Under Attack

Swann's cozy world is turned upside down when the *Black Pearl* launches an attack on Port Royal. Lured by the Gold Medallion that Elizabeth wears around her neck, the pirates storm the governor's mansion. By the time the governor returns to his wrecked home, his daughter is sailing from the port, a captive of Barbossa.

FORT IN FLAMES

Towering over the docks, Fort Charles guards Port Royal from pirate attack. At least, that's the idea. In fact, the fort has too few cannons. Its soldiers are better at drills and parades than warfare. The garrison finds it hard to defend itself; protecting the people of Port Royal as well is impossible. Pirates rule the Caribbean, and their ships are heavily armed. As cannon balls batter the stone walls of the fort, the ramparts are no place for dithering Governor Swann, who quakes with fear at every blast.

Armless Fun

When Barbossa's crew swarms aboard the *Dauntless*, Swann cowers in the captain's quarters. He is soon discovered by a bloodthirsty pirate and only just escapes his grasp. But Swann's ordeal isn't over; to his horror, during their skirmish, the arm of his cursed assailant comes off and has a life all of its own.

"ELIZABETH, ARE YOU THERE?"

On board the *Dauntless* Swann orders Elizabeth to remain in the captain's quarters and out of harm's way. But he underestimates his daughter's spirit and determination and discovers that she has escaped using knotted bedsheets so she can help Will.

Elizabeth Swann

In fine silk clothes, Elizabeth Swann looks every inch a lady. She plays the part of the perfect governor's daughter but secretly Port Royal society bores her. She dreads the thought of being a commodore's wife, respectable but dull. She dreams instead of a life of adventure. She cannot forget the moment eight years ago when she glimpsed a pirate ship on her voyage from England. At once both thrilling and frightening, it stood for everything she yearns for: excitement, danger, and freedom!

Hair elegantly swept up

Delicate antique lace trim

Tightly-laced corset beneath the dress makes it hard for Elizabeth to breathe

Sailing for Port Royal

Much to her father's dismay, pirates have always fascinated Elizabeth. As a girl on the voyage to Port Royal, she sang their songs. When the crew rescued a survivor from a pirate attack, she recognized the pirate Medallion he wore.

Wearing Aztec Gold

Elizabeth took the Medallion from young Will Turner so that the ship's crew would not guess he associated with pirates. She has kept it hidden ever since, but she doesn't realize the trouble it will bring.

A fan gives slight relief from the tropical sun

BREATHTAKING FASHIONS
Laced tightly into a corset and fashionable dress, Elizabeth feels suffocated. She's happier disguised in sailors' clothes that let her move easily.

Not Just a Pretty Face

Elizabeth is quick-witted and clever. When she goes aboard the *Black Pearl* to "Parlay" with Barbossa, she uses the Gold Medallion to strike a bargain. Her threat to drop it overboard makes the captain cooperate, but she soon finds she was foolish to trust him. Barbossa sails away, with Elizabeth still on board.

On Board the Terror Ship

In Elizabeth's dreams of an adventurous life she did not imagine herself being tossed in the air by a crew of skeletons. After her terrifying chase around the moonlit deck of the *Black Pearl,* she cowers in a corner of Barbossa's cabin.

Preparing for Battle

A challenge brings out the best in Elizabeth. With the *Black Pearl* in hot pursuit of the *Interceptor,* most women of her time would have taken cover. Instead Elizabeth is in the thick of the fighting. She takes command, figures out a way to turn the ship, and shouts "Fire all!" to start the battle.

Love and Loyalty

Above all, Elizabeth follows her heart. Marriage to Commodore Norrington would have brought her wealth and respect. But she would rather wed a humble blacksmith and become Mrs. Elizabeth Turner. Even her father realizes that he cannot persuade Elizabeth to change her mind.

Smoke Signals

Marooned with Captain Jack on a desert island, Elizabeth is horrified to discover that this bold pirate has no idea how to escape. While Jack drinks himself senseless, she burns his stock of rum. The huge fire alerts the navy, and they are rescued the next morning.

Will Turner

Until he met Jack Sparrow, swordsmith Will Turner was a simple craftsman. His life revolved around his work, and his distant longing for a woman he knew could never be his wife. But in a few short hours his world is turned upside down. He finds himself sucked into a nightmarish world of pirates, ghouls, adventure, and betrayal.

Will can throw an ax with amazing precision

Man Overboard!

Will first met Elizabeth when they were children and he was rescued after pirates attacked the ship on which he was sailing. Told to care for the half-drowned boy, Elizabeth immediately felt drawn to him—although she was worried when she found a pirate Medallion round his neck.

Simple jerkin

Bootstrap attached a chain to the Medallion so Will could wear it

MYSTERIOUS MEDALLION

Will believed his father was a respectable merchant seaman. When he gave Will an Aztec Medallion, his son thought it was just an exotic trinket that he had picked up on his travels. Will is shocked and dismayed when Jack reveals to him that his father was "Bootstrap Bill" Turner, "a good man, and a good pirate."

Ominous skull

Made for Each Other

Eight years after they met, Will is the man of Elizabeth's dreams. However, she does not dare tell him how she feels, for her father would never let them marry. A governor's daughter is too good for a lowly blacksmith!

Leather shoes with silver buckles

Proud Craftsman

In this dusty Port Royal smithy Will pumps the huge bellows and stokes the charcoal furnace. The furnace flames heat cold steel until it glows white hot. Forging a beautiful sword blade is punishing work: the many hours of hammering, folding, grinding, and polishing have given Will patience and strength.

ASLEEP ON THE JOB

Will's master is a man named John Brown. Although Brown is a drunk who seldom does any work, it is his forge and so his name decorates the swords Will makes. He takes the credit for catching Jack Sparrow too, after a lucky blow with an empty bottle.

Duel with a Pirate

Will is as handy with a blade as any soldier. He ought to be; after making the swords, he practices fencing with them for hours each day. When he discovers Jack in the forge, pirate captain and swordsmith are almost equally matched. "You know what you're doing, I'll give you that," quips Jack, who only manages to avoid losing to Will by acrobatic blade work—and old-fashioned cheating.

A LOYAL ALLY

When Jack faces the hangman, Will rushes to save his life—at great risk to his own. Though Will knows that he might be hanged as a pirate himself, he has a strong sense of what's right and what's not.

WILL'S SWORD

Unlike the ceremonial sword he made for Commodore Norrington's promotion, Will's weapon looks simple. It has a plain cast-iron grip, and a "half-basket" hilt protects his hand. The blade is special, though. By using the methods of Spanish swordsmiths, Will has made it immensely strong, yet light and flexible.

Will proudly engraved his own name on this blade

Blade has double-edged point for cutting and thrusting

Norrington

Loyal service to his majesty the king of England has brought James Norrington respect and status. As captain of HMS *Interceptor*, he has chased and captured some of the Caribbean's most fearsome pirates. He is promoted from Captain to Commodore of the Fleet, an advance that brings Norrington some satisfaction, but he still lacks the one thing that can bring him true happiness—taking Elizabeth Swann as his wife.

HMS *Interceptor*

Norrington's ship, the *Interceptor*, is perfect for chasing pirates in Caribbean waters. She is a brig and carries guns on two decks. Thanks to her fine lines she is fast and can turn quickly, but she's no match for the *Black Pearl*.

Loyal Officer

To maintain an air of authority, a captain in the English Navy cannot afford to show any emotion in front of his crew. Norrington has spent so many years masking his feelings that even in his personal affairs he is distant. Unfortunately for him, this is a trait that Elizabeth cannot bear.

MIXED–UP MARINES
Red-coated marines guard Norrington's ships. Unfortunately the bumbling Murtogg and Mullroy are more of a hindrance than a help.

GLEAMING STEEL
To mark his promotion, Norrington is given a new sword by Governor Swann. Beautifully hand-forged by Will Turner, it's perfectly balanced, and gold filigree decorates the handle.

On Parade

Norrington's promotion ceremony at the fort is a glittering military spectacle. Pipes and drums play. Sailors and marines march in perfect formation. Norrington himself is the star of the show. What better time to propose to Elizabeth? Unfortunately, her corset spoils everything, and she plunges swooning from the battlements into the sea.

DEATH SENTENCE

Norrington does not let sentiment get in the way of duty. The punishment for piracy on the high seas is death. Jack has also committed many other crimes—including impersonating a cleric of the Church of England—so the sentence is clear. Jack must hang. Norrington takes a pinch of snuff from his box, picks up his quill, and signs the warrant.

Dazzling and Desirable

The commodore is sure that he loves Elizabeth, but there are other reasons for marrying her. She can introduce him to important London families. And when her wealthy father dies, Elizabeth will inherit a small fortune.

BEATEN IN LOVE...

When Elizabeth stands by Will in protecting Jack, Norrington knows his rival in love has beaten him. He accepts defeat nobly, telling Will "This is a beautiful sword. I would expect the man who made it to show the same care in every aspect of his life."

... AND IN LIFE

After Jack escapes from Port Royal, recapturing him becomes a mission that takes over Norrington. He chases the pirate all over the world, until he makes a fatal mistake. In pursuit of Jack he orders his crew to sail through a hurricane, wrecking his ship. He is fired from the navy for his foolishness, and becomes a penniless drunk.

Pirates Beware!

After his capture, Jack Sparrow is given a room looking out across Port Royal bay. Unfortunately, prison bars somewhat spoil the view. It's not the first time Jack has been locked up, but he's worried, nonetheless. Imprisonment is the beginning of a story that soon ends, with "a short drop and a sudden stop," for the punishment for piracy is the hangman's noose. Inside Port Royal's prison, Jack thinks about this hazard, but he does not give up hope. After all, he has cheated the hangman before. Why should this time be any different?

Jailer with a Tail

Jack takes one look at his doggy jailer and decides that he is no more likely to hand over the keys than a human guard. "The dog is never going to move," he tells his fellow prisoners as they try and lure the hound within reach with a bone.

"I Know Those Guns!"

The sound of gunfire makes Jack Sparrow spring from his hard stone seat to gaze at the bay. Although his prison cell is directly in the firing line, the blasts are music to his ears, for he quickly recognizes the sound of the guns as those of his beloved *Black Pearl*.

BOUND FOR THE GALLOWS
Jack's criminal companions are desperate to avoid the hangman. Though they can't tempt the prison dog, a cannonball sets them free. As they escape though a hole in their cell wall they sympathize with Jack, still locked inside: "You've no manner of luck at all," they tell him.

THE
TRYALS
OF
PIRATES, *Viz.*

Peter Marshall,
James Kiley, *other* Killa
Courtney Anderson,
Charles Stewart,
...es Robinson,

Ernest Lauterio,
Scott Bailey,
David Gordon,
Mark Davies,
Larry Dias

Condemn'd for PIRACY, *at the Town of*
...within His Majesty's Province in Jamaica,
...by several Adjournments

VOLUNTEERS
God Save the King

Able SEAMEN
Of OLD ENGLAND

They will be allowed to Enter... Naval War
and the following BOUNTIES will be... by his MAJESTY
IN Addition to The... Months Advance.

To Able Seamen,
To Ordinary Seamen,
To Landmen,

Death Sentence

This time, Jack keeps his appointment with the hangman. Moments away from death, he can't help smiling as he remembers some of the crimes the town clerk reads out: "... impersonating a cleric of the Church of England... sailing under false colors... arson... depravity…." His smile fades as the list ends "...you are sentenced to be hung by the neck until dead...."

A Narrow Escape

Just as Jack is beginning to think that his luck has finally run out, Will dashes to the rescue. He draws his sword, and hurls it at the very moment that the hangman pulls the lever to execute Jack. By standing on Will's blade, Jack stops the noose from tightening around his neck.

PIRATES
YE BE
WARNED

A simple wooden sign accompanies the swaying bodies

A GRUESOME DISPLAY

Commodore Norrington shows off the bodies of executed pirates near the dock. He hopes that this grisly spectacle will encourage passing sailors to obey the law. To preserve the corpses, they are lightly boiled in seawater and dipped in tar before being put on display.

Black Pearl

With sails as dark as a moonless night, and a hull painted to match, the *Black Pearl* is every inch a pirate ship. She's built for action, too: behind the gunports on each side are two rows of deadly cannons. Sailing the *Pearl* demands teamwork, skill, and strength. The crew works together to stretch the tattered sails tight against the gusty wind. When danger threatens, they'll fight to the death to defend themselves and their beloved ship.

Who's in Charge?

Pirate ships have captains, just as naval ships do, but pirates obey only the orders they agree with! Sailors on the *Pearl* vow to uphold the Pirate Code. But the rules it contains are more like guidelines: the crew can even change their captain if they don't like him.

NAVIGATION

Though Jack often lets his special compass guide him, he navigates just as other seamen do. Near coasts, he relies on charts (sea maps.) Far from land, he uses an instrument called a sextant to measure the sun's height at noon. From this he can calculate how far he's sailed north or south.

Wooden tube makes the spyglass light and easy to handle

SPYGLASS

Spotting distant ships and shores at sea isn't easy—even from the crow's nest. So mariners use a spyglass (telescope) nicknamed the "bring-em-closer" to magnify the view.

The Only Woman on Board

Like all mariners, pirates are a superstitious
bunch, and they believe that women on board a
ship will always bring bad luck. They make one
exception: wooden women are allowed, but only
if they are nailed to the bow as a figurehead.
The *Black Pearl*'s figurehead shows a beautiful
woman with an outstretched arm and a bird
about to take flight from her hand.

*There are no flush lavatories
on a pirate ship! Instead, the
crew takes advantage of the
"seats of ease"—holes in the
deck behind the figurehead,
with seats mounted above*

*Mariners
believe the eyes
of the figurehead
help their ship to
find its way at sea*

LOADING FOOD
Fresh food is a luxury on the *Pearl*
because it soon rots in the tropical
heat. Mostly the crew live on hard
tack (biscuits) and salted meat.
The captain eats better and the
ship carries a few live sheep and
chickens for his table.

SHIP'S SUPPLIES
To load supplies into the hold
at the very bottom of the ship,
the crew lowers them down a
hatchway. For heavier supplies
they use the yards as cranes.

NIGHTY-NIGHT SHIPMATES!
The *Pearl*'s crew sleep on deck, or in hammocks below
when the weather is bad. With the gunports closed,
there is little ventilation, and the air at night quickly
turns foul. Sailors wake with a horrid taste in their
mouths as though they have been sucking on a penny.

Barbossa

Ruthless and cunning, Barbossa has one aim: to become mortal once more. He leads his crew in search of gold and blood to lift the Aztec curse. Without them, Barbossa cannot die—but can never truly live. It is a punishment he deserves, for Barbossa rose through the ranks, and through treachery and cruelty he swiftly became captain. Barbossa signed on as first mate on the *Black Pearl*. The mutiny he led robbed Captain Jack Sparrow of his ship.

Blue ostrich feathers show Barbarossa's vanity

Grudge Match

Barbossa marooned the overthrown captain, Jack Sparrow, on a desert island. Barbossa gave Jack a gun with just one shot—to kill himself when heat and thirst got too much. So Barbossa is amazed when Jack reappears.

A ROVING EYE

Barbossa thinks Elizabeth's blood will help him lift the curse, but he is also attracted by her beauty. Perhaps she'd make him a fine pirate bride?

No Mercy!

Once Barbossa realizes that it is Will's blood he really needs, Elizabeth is worthless to him. He doesn't hesitate to make her walk the plank, to face the sharks—or a slower death on a barren island.

Buttons made from melted down Inca silver stolen from Spanish ships

Decorative and Deadly

With his flintlock, Barbossa deals out death like a gentleman. He won the elegantly engraved gun when a Spanish pirate challenged him to a duel. His foolish opponent lost his pistol as well as his life.

Old but Powerful

Barbossa is old enough to be the father of some members of his crew, but none question his authority. Even when they blame him for the Aztec curse, Barbossa's legendary skill with a sword makes sure he remains their chief.

Barbossa's Ring

Plundered from a Venetian ship, Barbossa's ring shows a lion's head—the symbol of a leader.

Flesh to Bones

As Barbossa steps from his cabin onto the moonlit deck, Elizabeth at last sees him as the phantom that he really is. "You'd best start believing in ghost stories, Miss Turner..." the living corpse tells her "...you're in one!"

The Cursed Crew

Scoundrels and scallywags, murderers and malefactors, drunkards and desperadoes sail the *Black Pearl*. In other words, the ship has a crew of perfectly ordinary pirates. Or they would be ordinary, if they were not cursed like their captain. To end the curse, they will follow Barbossa anywhere. Their quest has taken them so long that—like the sails—their clothes are in tatters, and salt crusts their hair. With their attack on Port Royal, the pirates sense that they will soon be leaving the world of the living dead. For the last Gold piece and the blood of "Bootstrap Bill" are almost within reach.

Pintel practices his famous scowl in front of a mirror

All Hands on Deck!

The members of the *Black Pearl's* crew come from a dozen nations, and include escaped slaves from West Africa and Hispaniola. Most were once privateers—sailors who plundered enemy vessels during wartime. When peace returned, they lost their jobs and were lured into piracy.

Washing clothes in chamberlye (urine) after a battle gets out the worst of the blood stains

Fashionable large-buckled leather shoe

MONKEY BUSINESS
The smallest member of the crew is also one of the most useful. Named "Jack" after Jack Sparrow, Barbossa's pet monkey takes care of the precious Gold Medallion. He carries it far out of reach in the rigging when danger threatens.

Dim-witted Duo

Pintel and Ragetti are cutthroat pirates but more often than not their lack of common sense and their constant bickering make them the clowns of Barbossa's crew. They were pressed into service by the English Navy, but jumped ship after a year of beatings, bad food, and boredom and eventually found themselves on board the *Black Pearl*.

Ragetti lost his eye in battle. The wooden replacement "splinters 'somefink' terrible."

Jacket stolen from a French nobleman

DEVIOUS DISGUISES

It is Pintell and Ragetti that Barbossa chooses to create a diversion while the rest of the crew walks out to the *Dauntless*: "This is just like what the Greeks done at Troy... 'cept they was in a horse, 'stead of dresses."

SWARMING ABOARD

The *Pearl's* crew meet fierce resistance as they swing across to the *Interceptor*. They are not used to such opposition. Crews attacked by pirates—even flesh-and-blood pirates—usually give in without a battle.

Explosive!

Homemade grenades help to spread panic and confusion during the pirates' attacks. The bombs are made from pottery globes stuffed with gunpowder and explode with lots of smoke and noise.

Caked-on tar gives pants extra water resistance—and a pungent odor

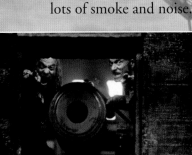

FIRING A BROADSIDE

Barbossa waits until the *Interceptor* is alongside before ordering the crew to fire. Cannons are not accurate enough to hit distant targets, and like most pirates, the *Pearl's* crew is too disorganized to make good use of them.

Curse of the Aztec Gold

Doomed by their greed, the *Black Pearl*'s cursed crew regrets the day it found the Gold. At first the men laughed at stories that it was cursed. They could believe that Hernando Cortés, the Spanish conquistador, had once owned it. Maybe it was true that Mexico's Aztec rulers used it to bribe Cortés, to stop him looting their country. But the curse? "Ridiculous superstition!" said Barbossa. Alas, he was wrong, and by the time he learned the truth, it was too late.

Phantom Captain

When Barbossa steps into the moonlight, the grim effects of the curse are plain to see. The flesh vanishes from his bones, and he becomes a walking skeleton. To lift the curse, Barbossa must return every piece of Aztec Gold to the stone chest from which it came—and add the blood of "Bootstrap Bill."

Rotting flesh hangs from his bleached white rib bones

Moonlight turns Barbossa's fine clothes to rags

Apple Agony

Barbossa and his crew suffer a living death, feeling and tasting nothing: "...drink would not satisfy; food turned to ash in our mouths." The pirate captain is tormented by flavorless apples. He longs to be mortal, so that he can once more taste the flesh of the fruit, and feel the juice running down his chin.

Cursed Crew

Pintel and Ragetti are cursed like the others, wandering the world as skeletons that cannot be killed. Their longing to lift the curse has given them a sixth sense, that lures them to the Gold pieces. "The Gold calls to us," they tell Elizabeth as they find her with the Aztec Medallion in the governor's house.

Dauntless, moored in the shallows off the coast of *Isla de Muerta*, they simply walk upon the sea bed and climb up the ship's anchor.

blood, into the chest. Human once more, Barbossa dies.

A TABLE OF TREATS
On board the *Black Pearl*, the pirates look forward to becoming human again. Like Barbossa, they long to taste food once more, and fantasize about what they will eat first when the curse is lifted.

A Motley Crew

Of all the pirate islands in the Caribbean, none is the equal of Tortuga. Dangerous, boisterous, drunken, and bawdy, Tortuga is pirate heaven. So it's no surprise that when Captain Jack Sparrow is looking for a crew, he steers a course here. Named by the Spanish after the turtle it resembles, the island lies to the north of Hispaniola. It is far enough from civilization to escape attention, but close to the route the treasure ships sail. Surely Jack will find men crazy enough to join him on his dangerous adventure here.

A Worthy First Mate

Jack quickly finds a loyal first mate, sleeping in a pig sty. Joshamee Gibbs is an old friend. He served in the Royal Navy for a while but Jack forgave him for this because he deserted his post and turned pirate once more.

JACK'S LEVERAGE

Will thinks that Jack is leading him to Elizabeth because he freed Jack from jail, and because he knew his father. However, when Will hears Jack refer to him as his "leverage," he begins to suspect that he only knows half the story.

RELUCTANT PIRATE

The crew member with the least experience of all is Will himself. For a blacksmith, however, he turns out to be a pretty good sailor. Once he gets over his seasickness, he learns to scamper up the rigging as nimbly as any midshipman. Jack is not surprised; he knows that with "Bootstrap Bill" for a father, Will has piracy in his blood.

Crew on Parade

"Feast your eyes, Captain! All of them faithful hands before the mast...," Gibbs tells Jack as he parades the crew. Will doubts their skill, but Jack doesn't mind. He knows that sailors have to be either crazy or stupid to sign up for the kind of mission he has in mind.

Speechless

Cotton doesn't reply when Jack asks him whether he has the courage and fortitude to join the crew—he can't because his tongue has been cut out. "Wind in your sails!" Cotton's parrot replies for him. "We figure that means 'Yes,'" explains Gibbs.

Angry Anamaria

At the end of the line a crew member with a large hat asks in a suspiciously high-pitched voice "What's the benefit for us?" It's Anamaria, and she believes that Jack has a debt to repay. "You stole my boat!" she accuses him, adding a couple of slaps for emphasis. Jack admits he deserves them, but he can hardly return the boat now. After all, it's sitting at the bottom of Port Royal harbor.

Stormy Weather

The crew faces its first test when a ferocious storm hits the ship. Despite striking all but the mainsail, the *Interceptor* is swamped by the mountainous waves. United by danger, the crew battle with the storm and survive.

The Crew Sees Action

When the *Black Pearl* starts to chase the *Interceptor*, Jack's crew really shows what they can do. Elizabeth's ignorance of sailing helps; her insane ideas help them gain some speed and win vital minutes to prepare for battle. But once they have thrown all the cannonballs overboard, what are they going to fire from the guns? "Case shot and langrage! Nails and crushed glass!" orders Gibbs. When they open fire on the *Black Pearl*, Ragetti is the first to taste this strange ammunition—a fork hits his wooden eye.

Taking the Lead

Elizabeth discovers to her dismay that the crew really does follow the pirate code of "he who falls behind gets left behind." They won't follow her to *Isla de Muerta* to rescue Will. All she can do is to launch the boat herself and row back alone.

Isla de Meutra

What better place to hide treasure than an island that cannot be found—except by those who know where it is? *Isla de Muerta*, or "Island of the Dead," is just such a place. It was to here that Barbossa sailed using the bearings he had tricked out of Jack Sparrow. It was in the echoing cave here on the island that Barbossa found the stone chest of Aztec Gold. And it's to the same stone chest that the crew of the *Black Pearl* return the 882 pieces of Aztec gold as they find them, one by one.

Strange Kind of Treasure

The pirates don't just bring the Aztec Gold to *Isla de Muerta*; they heap up all their plunder in the cave. Until the curse is lifted, wealth is worthless to them, for nothing they can buy brings them pleasure. Not everything in the cave is valuable: Pintel and Ragetti mistakenly bring a trunk of women's clothes.

PILE IT HIGH
Packed in chests, and heaped in messy piles, gold and silver fill the cave. Precious jewels are strewn across the ground.

Pearl string once hung around the neck of a princess of Bavaria

Amethyst centerpiece of brooch is big as pigeon's egg

PEARLS AND JEWELS
The treasure on *Isla de Muerta* includes huge quantities of gold and silver bars and coins. They came from raids on Spanish ships heading back to Seville from the country's colonies in Mexico and Peru. But some of the most valuable pieces are jewelry stolen from wealthy passengers on ships the *Black Pearl* attacked.

Lifting the Curse

Barbossa's crew brings Elizabeth to the island to return the last coin that she wears around her neck. They also aim to cut her with a flint knife. They think she's the daughter of "Bootstrap Bill" and her blood will lift the curse—but they are wrong. She lied about who she was, giving Will's Turner's last name.

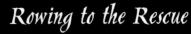

Rowing to the Rescue

Jack and Will follow the crew of the *Black Pearl* to the island. From their hiding place, they helplessly watch as Barbossa prepares to sacrifice Elizabeth. When Jack won't stop the ceremony, Will suspects that Jack doesn't care what happens to her. He knocks Jack unconscious with an oar, and plucks Elizabeth to safety.

STABBED IN THE BACK
A skeleton with a sword in its back gives Will the idea that Jack is about to betray him.

We Have an Accord!

Captain Sparrow may be devious, but he's not a traitor—despite what Will believes. When Barbossa returns to *Isla de Muerta* to spill Will's blood, Jack proposes a partnership. "Wait to lift the curse until the opportune moment," he tells Barbossa. His canny deal saves Will's life.

Wedding Bells

White lace, flowers, a flowing dress, and an altar. Everything is in place to make Elizabeth's wedding day perfect, except for one detail—the groom. Dark clouds fill the sky, and tears fill the bride's eyes. Surely Will would not let her down? Finally, as tropical rain soaks her bridal gown, Elizabeth learns the truth. Port Royal has a new boss. Her husband-to-be is in chains, accused of helping a pirate to escape, and Elizabeth is charged with the same crime.

Beautiful golden gown ruined by rain

Unexpected Arrival

The cause of Elizabeth's misery is Lord Cutler Beckett, of the East India Trading Company. Clever and devious, he has become more powerful even than Governor Swann. Using his emergency powers "to rid the seas of piracy," he takes control of Port Royal.

Shackled!

Arrested as he dresses for his wedding, Will Turner arrives at the chapel in chains. Beckett reads out the charges against him: "...conspiring to set free a man lawfully convicted of crimes against the Empire, and condemned to death. For which the penalty is... death."

The heavy raindrops knock the petals from her bouquet, and the smile from her face

WET WEDDING

As if being stood up at the altar isn't enough, a rainstorm wrecks Elizabeth's wedding plans. Palm trees bend as the gale-force winds scatter chairs, and the guests run for cover. Elizabeth can't believe that Will would not show up, and she sinks to her knees on the sodden grass.

UNINVITED GUESTS

Lord Cutler Beckett's men take no chances. They surround the chapel where Elizabeth slumps in her soaking bridal gown. "My apologies for arriving without an invitation..."

BAFFLED BRIDE

Hoisted to her feet by soldiers, Elizabeth cannot quite understand what's going on. When she turns to see Will in chains she realizes that he has been arrested—and her dream of marrying the man she loves lies in tatters.

SILK SHOES

Elizabeth's wedding shoes are made from fine Chinese silk, with details picked out in tiny freshwater pearls. They match her dress and train perfectly, but rubber boots would have been better suited to her wedding-day weather.

Under Arrest!

Beckett's arrival with Will shocks Governor Swann. "By what authority have you arrested this man?" he demands. "By the Crown's authority," Beckett replies, and he has a pile of documents to prove it. Sure enough, Will's name is on a warrant, and he cannot deny that he is guilty. There's another warrant for Elizabeth, and one for Norrington, too.

In Search of Jack

When Will sets off in search of Jack Sparrow, he holds out no great hope of finding him. After all, Jack could be anywhere, and even the Royal Navy wasn't able to catch him. Will searches all over the Caribbean. The clues he finds lead him to a remote island... and terrible danger.

WHERE THERE'S A WILL THERE'S A WAY

When Will visits his jailed bride, he tells her Beckett has offered a deal: Elizabeth will go free if Will tracks down Jack. Will has no choice but to accept—though neither of them trust Beckett to keep his word.

Lord Beckett

As supreme head of the East India Trading Company, Lord Cutler Beckett is a man with a mission. He aims to stamp out piracy wherever he finds it on the high seas. He has come to Port Royal to capture and execute scoundrels such as Jack Sparrow and the crew of the *Black Pearl*. He will do whatever he thinks is necessary to achieve his goal.

Beckett Beckons!

Although he pretends that he is interested only in stamping out piracy, Beckett has one more reason to capture Jack Sparrow. He knows all about the Dead Man's Chest, and about the heart of Davy Jones that beats inside it. Beckett believes that Jack Sparrow will lead him to the chest. Then he can control Davy Jones—and eliminate pirates from the Seven Seas.

Mercer

Beckett arrives in Port Royal accompanied by his faithful assistant, Mercer. On the face of it Mercer is a clerk like any other—efficient, obedient, and loyal, but he has a more sinister side. When doing his master's dirty work he is cruel and menacing and uses underhand tactics, stopping at nothing to aid Beckett's pursuit of power.

STORMY ARRIVAL
Beckett uses his arrival in Port Royal to show how powerful he is. Royal Navy ships seal off the harbor. Marines march in step along the dock. Beckett himself is rowed ashore astride a white horse. He times his arrival so that he will interrupt Will and Elizabeth's wedding. He knows he can use them as bait to snare Jack.

Swann Defeated

Caught helping his daughter to flee the island, Governor Swann is imprisoned. Swann assumes that Beckett wants to govern Port Royal himself. But Beckett is more clever than Swann had realized. He wants Swann to stay on as governor but wants him to send good reports to his bosses in London in exchange for Elizabeth's safety.

BRANDED

Beckett brands pirates with a "P." This branding iron glows red hot once heated in a fire and allows him to inflict his special kind of punishment. He presses the searing letter onto the forearm of pirates he captures, leaving them permanently scarred.

The tip of the cane was used to brand Jack Sparrow

Pirate's License

Beckett knows that Jack will not want to hand over his compass so in exchange he offers him Letters of Marque. Signed by the king of England, these documents would make Jack a licensed pirate. His earlier crimes would be forgiven and he could legally attack the ships of any nation at war with England.

Beckett has yet to fill in Jack's name on the letters

Royal seal and signature of King George

Leather wallet protects documents

Beckett's seal and signature

Safety device stops gun from going off by mistake

POCKET PISTOL

Beckett has made many enemies during his rise to power. Some would cheerfully kill him. To protect himself Beckett carries a pistol. Its short barrel allows him to slip it easily into a specially made pocket in the lining of his frock coat.

Beckett's Plan

Lord Cutler Beckett is a loyal member of the East India Trading Company. He has great ambitions for the company and has a map of the world painted on his office wall to illustrate them. To further the achievements of the company he aims to rid the seas of piracy by finding the Dead Man's Chest. Then he can control Davy Jones himself, and rule every ship, sailor, and creature of the Seven Seas.

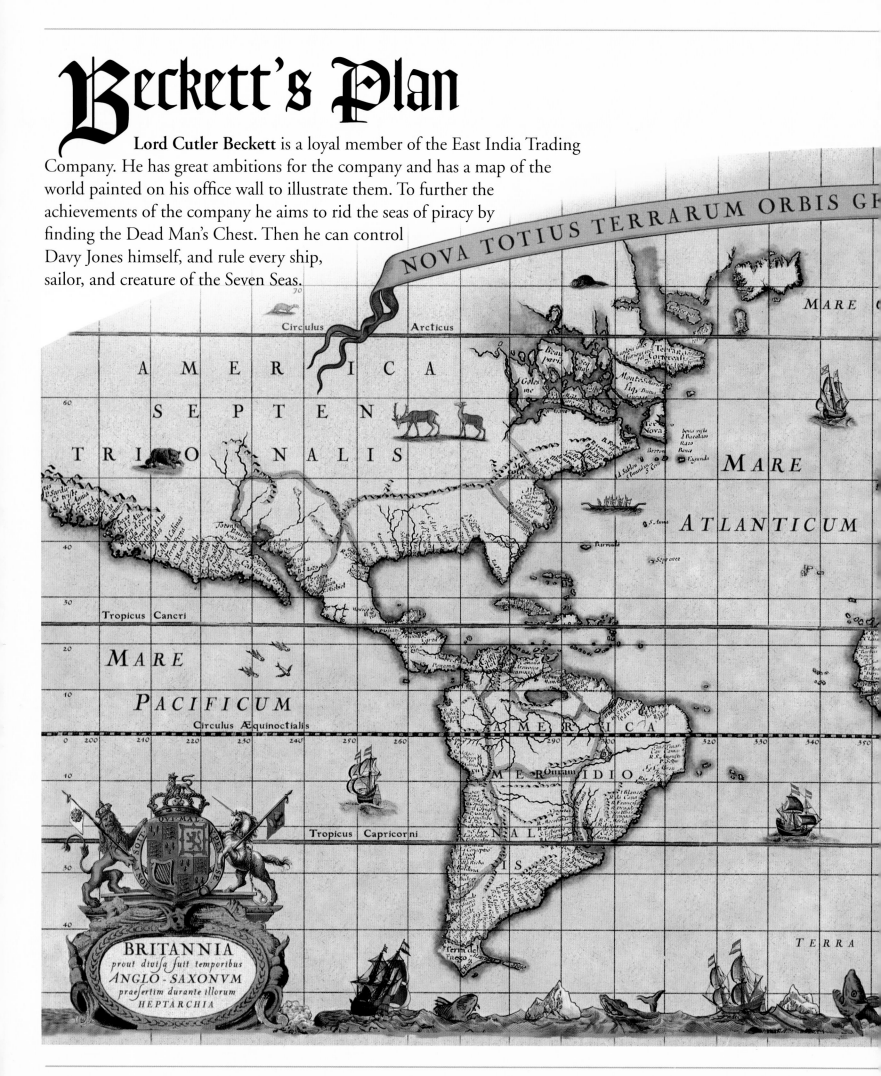

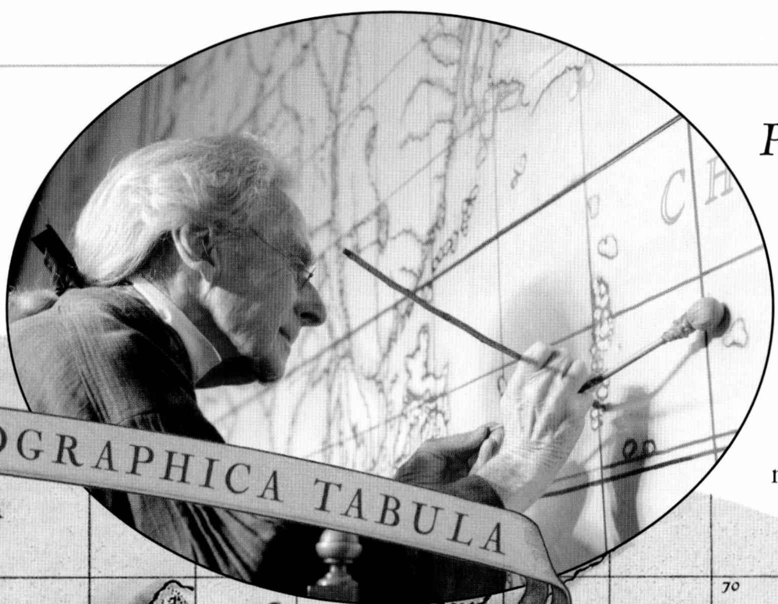

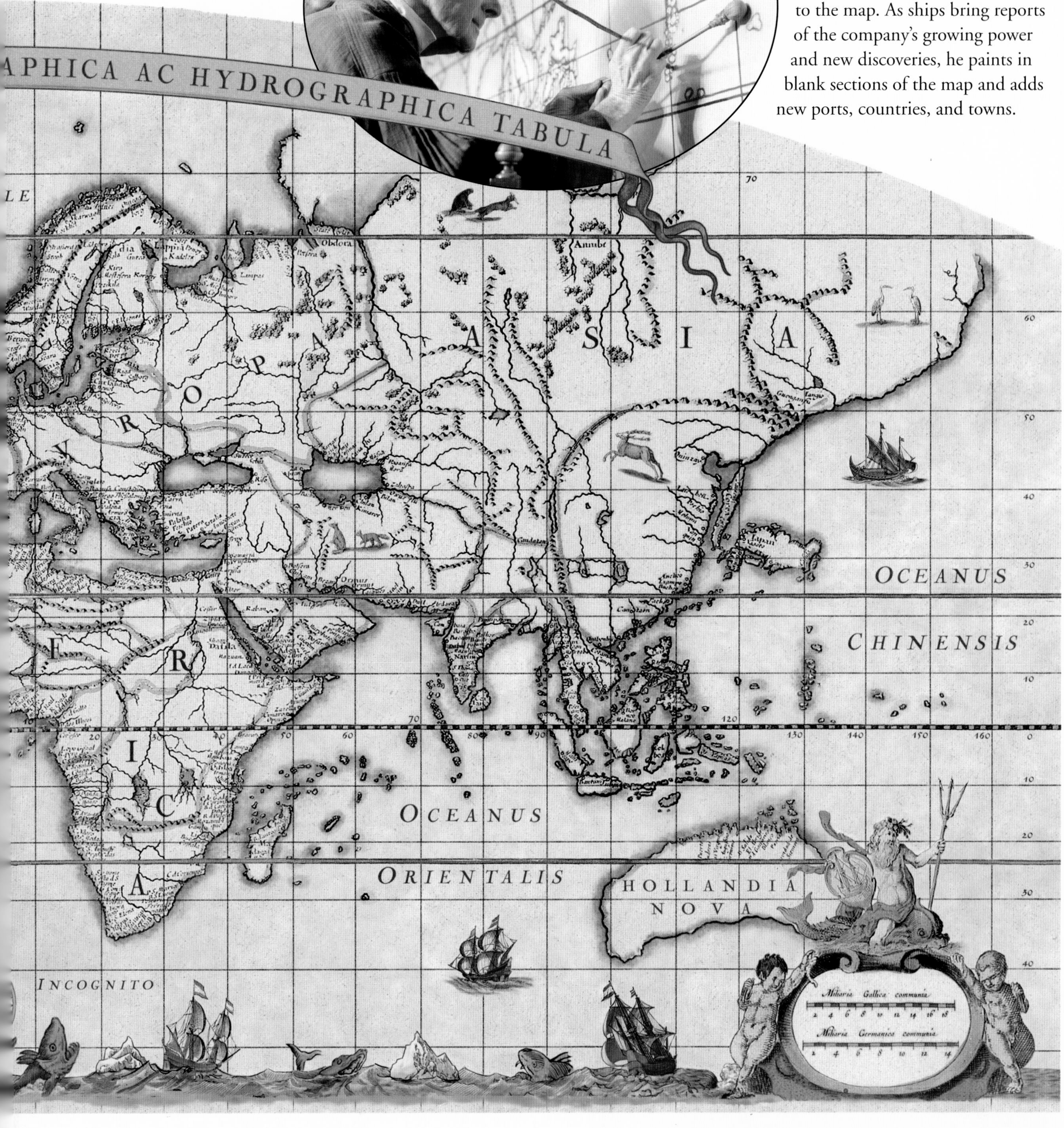

APHICA AC HYDROGRAPHICA TABULA
LE
A S I A
V R O P A
F R I C A
OCEANUS
CHINENSIS
OCEANUS
ORIENTALIS
HOLLANDIA
NOVA
INCOGNITO
Miliaria Gallica communia
Miliaria Germanica communia

Painting in the Corners

Beckett's plans need to be constantly updated. He employs an artisan to make daily changes to the map. As ships bring reports of the company's growing power and new discoveries, he paints in blank sections of the map and adds new ports, countries, and towns.

East India Trading Co.

When European explorers first sailed to the East Indies, they were hypnotized by the fabulous wealth they found. The gold, silver, ivory, silk, and exotic spices lured traders hungry for a profit. English merchants were particularly successful in sponsoring trading voyages. The East India Trading Company, the company they set up, grew in size and power and controlled much of India's trade. Eager to expand still further, the powerful men at the head of the company now looked to the rich plantations of the Caribbean.

LORD CUTLER BECKETT
Ambitious and ruthless, Cutler Beckett is in the Caribbean to oversee the expansion. He would be delighted to change the company's name to the East and West India Trading Company. But he knows that he can make no progress until he has stamped out the scourge of piracy.

COAT OF ARMS
The company's gold and maroon coat of arms shows how grand its goals are. Beneath waving pennants, sea lions support a shield dotted with ships and roses. The Latin slogan on a ribbon underneath means "Nothing can harm us when God leads us."

Loading Up

Tied up at Port Royal docks, an East India Trading Company ship loads up. Sugar—as sugar loaves or molasses—fills most of her hold, and barrels of rum much of the remainder. But there's still room for a bewildering variety of other goods to trade between the islands.

Derricks lower heavy cargo into the hold

Company uses much smaller ships in the Caribbean than the huge East Indiamen that sail to India

Boxes, Bundles, and Bales

Once the ship's officers have completed the company's business at the ports they visit, they are allowed to do a little trading on their own account. (They do a little smuggling, too, even though it's strictly forbidden.) Along the docks the merchants and farmers of Port Royal line up to load the officer's purchases.

Send in the Marines!

The East India Trading Company has grown so large that a threat to the company is a threat to Britain itself. So the government takes care to protect the company, supplying marines to guard its ships and a Royal Navy escort when dangerous pirates such as Jack Sparrow are abroad.

EAST INDIA TRADING Co

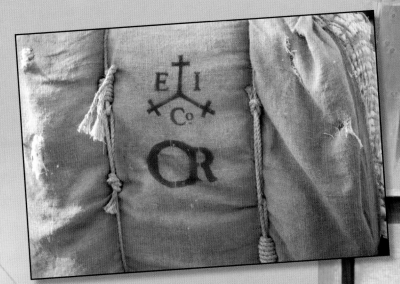

COMPANY TRADEMARK

Stamped, stenciled, and painted on every box, bundle, and barrel loaded aboard the ship is the trademark of the East India Trading Company. Separated by triple crosses, the company's initials act as a guarantee of quality—and also discourage petty thieves.

Wooden crate contains colorful silk from the Far East, a luxury prized in the Caribbean

Jack's Bargain

Pirates never buy their ships. Some "borrow" them. Most steal them. A few trade them in crooked deals. The *Black Pearl*, however, is like no other ship, and Jack Sparrow is no ordinary pirate. What brought them together was a dark and dangerous bargain. Thirteen years ago Jack made a deal with Davy Jones. The commander of the oceans raised the *Black Pearl* from the depths in exchange for Jack's soul. Now the time has come for Jack to keep his side of the bargain.

Seashells and barnacles grow from his face

Davy Jones' Messenger

In a strange twist of fate it is Will's father, "Bootstrap Bill," who brings Jack the bad news. After Bootstrap was sent overboard by Barbossa, Davy Jones offered to save him if he pledged to serve on the *Flying Dutchman* for a century. Ever since, Bill has been a helpless crewman for the ocean's ruler.

NIGHTMARE

At first Jack thinks he's had too much rum. He goes to look for another bottle, and finds it encrusted with barnacles. Inside, there's only sand. It's when Bootstrap appears from the shadows that Jack begins to get really surprised. "Is this a dream?" he asks, hoping he'll wake up soon.

TIME TO SETTLE A DEBT

Bootstrap reminds Jack of his bargain with Davy Jones saying "the terms what applied to me applied to you, too: one soul, bound to crew upon his ship for a lifetime." Either Jack must give himself up or Jones' sea beast will deliver him to its master.

Jack tells Bootstrap that Will helped him win back the *Black Pearl*. Bill's delighted that his son "ended up a pirate after all...."

Barnacles cling to the handle and guard

BOOTSTRAP'S SWORD

Though it's forged from the native iron of the seabed, Bootstrap's sword does not look like much. A thick coating of rust has dulled and blunted the once-gleaming blade. However, in Bill's hands it's a lethal weapon. He swings it with truly terrifying power, cutting through heavy ships' beams as if they were seaweed.

The Black Spot

Jack is a marked man after his visit from "Bootstrap Bill." Staring at his hand in horror, he sees the Black Spot appear in the middle of his palm. It's a sign that Davy Jones' obedient sea beast will find him wherever he flees on the Seven Seas. The merciless Kraken will drag Jack down to Davy Jones' Locker.

Cannibal Island

In the most remote corner of the Caribbean sea lies a mysterious island. It is missing from ocean charts and far from all normal shipping routes. Its warlike people, the Pelegostos, have a grim secret: they relish the taste of "long pig"—human flesh. It is to this very island that the unfortunate Jack Sparrow flees when he is cursed with the BLACK SPOT!

Rickety bridges made from jungle vines allow the cannibals to cross the gaping ravines that carve up the island

CANNIBAL CLAN
Painted, pierced, masked, and, above all, hungry, the cannibals make a fearsome sight. Their carefully applied face and body paint isn't just decorative. It makes them blend in perfectly with the dripping tropical rain forest that covers their island home. For weapons they use spears, machetes, and blow pipes with drugged darts.

HOME SWEET HOME
Woven from plant fibers, the cannibal huts look like the homes of funnel-web spiders. Despite their fragile appearance, they provide shelter from heavy tropical storms.

DANCE OF DEATH
Half ballet, half funeral march, this tribal dance celebrates a hearty meal. They dance with a special frenzy: Jack Sparrow is on the menu, and by eating him (they believe) they will turn him from human to god.

WASTE NOT, WANT NOT
This bone pile is not just leftovers. The tops of skulls make useful drinking cups and eye sockets neatly hold candles upright.

The village is built on the flat top of one of the island's soaring peaks

The Pelegostos Tribe

Will follows Jack to a remote and apparently deserted island. He senses he is in terrible danger when the pilot of the shrimp boat that ferries him there is a little too eager to get away. As Will steps onto the beach there is an eerie silence, broken only when Cotton's parrot lands on a tree squawking "Don't eat me!" As Will hacks his way inland contemplating the parrot's peculiar words, little does he realize he's walking straight into a trap.

Rain-forest Raiders

Will does not see the crouching figures that lie in wait for him. The patterns of their body painting form a perfect camouflage against the background of leaves and creepers. He is captured before he even realizes he's being watched.

RELUCTANT LEADER
The Pelegostos tribe has adopted Jack as its king! He is given a grim necklace made from toes and his face is painted with four pairs of scary staring eyes.

ON THE THRONE
Jack sits on a grand throne decorated with skulls and bones at the heart of the cannibal village. He has picked up the local language and talks to his subjects in grunts, clicks, and teeth-grinding sounds.

Will on a Stick

Once they have captured Will, the hunters truss him up like an animal and carry him to their village. There, Will is delighted to see Jack, and assumes he will soon be free. But when Jack pretends not to recognize him and whispers, "Save me!" Will realizes that he and Jack face the same gruesome fate.

Badges of Royalty

As cannibal king, Jack gets to wear a special necklace of human toes. His feather scepter commands all who see it to obey him (as long as he doesn't ask for freedom.)

Sinews hold the feathers in place

Grisly toe garland

The Crew Escapes

Though they are trapped inside a cage made out of human bones, Will and the crew of the *Black Pearl* manage to escape, taking their prison with them. They make a dash for the beach, the ship, and freedom!

Sparrow Kebab

Before the cannibals can barbecue him, Jack escapes too. The wooden stake tied to his back makes a handy vaulting pole, springing him across a jungle ravine.

Sprint for the Ship

Just as the *Black Pearl* sets sail, Captain Jack Sparrow dashes down the beach and jumps on board. The cannibals will need to find a new dinner "guest."

The Bayou

Jack Sparrow realizes he will need help to track down Davy Jones. So he goes looking for someone he knows he can rely on, voodoo priestess Tia Dalma. The journey to the tumbledown shack where she lives is not an easy one. Jack, Will, and the crew have to find their way through a spooky cypress forest. They launch two longboats from the *Black Pearl*, and cautiously paddle up the Pantano River. As they venture farther into the forest a sense of unease descends upon them as the tall trees block out the sunlight, alligators stir on mud banks, and the curious swamp people watch them silently from the riverbanks.

Tree House

Tia Dalma's shack clings to the branches of a tree in a distant part of the swamp. Though it glows brightly, the hut seems to suck the light out of the surrounding forest. Every kind of lumber makes up the walls and roof. In between the forest logs are nailed planks from coffins, and parts of discarded canoes patch the roof.

"HAVE A GOOD TRIP!"

Jack doesn't like the journey through the forest at all. Though he seems to know where he is going, he keeps a tight grip on the rope, and glances around himself nervously all the time. His traveling companions are just as frightened. They are worried about Jack, too. "What is it that has Jack spooked?" asks Will. "Nothing can keep Jack Sparrow from the sea."

FOREST BEASTS

The crew stares wide-eyed at the strangely colored reptiles that scuttle nimbly along the branches of the trees.

SILENT AUDIENCE

Though the people of the swamp do them no harm, Jack and the others get nervous just from being watched so closely. A pair of eyes seems to peer at them from every shadow. They are not so worried by the figures they can see clearly, like this old man sitting in a rocking chair on his porch, with a dog at his feet. It's what they can't see clearly that they fear most, such as the figures half hidden in the leaves.

UP THE LADDER

At Tia Dalma's shack, a ladder leads up from the water, and Jack climbs it. "Tia Dalma and I go way back," he brags. "Thick as thieves. Nigh inseparable, we were. I'll handle this." Though he puts on a brave face, he's not sure of himself, and whispers "guard my back" to Gibbs.

SPOOKY PROCESSION

When the meeting is over, Jack's crew follows him down the ladder and clambers gratefully into the canoes. They have an uncanny feeling that this won't be their last visit to the cypress forest. Though each of them silently swears that they will never return to this creepy place, they all know that they can't cheat destiny.

Tia Dalma's Shack

Perched in a treetop by the mouth of the Pantano River is a shack belonging to voodoo priestess, Tia Dalma. It is a damp and gloomy world where nothing is quite what it seems to be. However, judging Tia Dalma by her humble home is a mistake. She has uncanny powers to foretell the future, to summon up demons, and to look deep into men's souls. So it's to this mysterious and beautiful priestess that Jack turns when he wants to find Davy Jones.

Claw Reading

Tia Dalma has amazing abilities and uses them to help her old friend Jack. With a clatter of crab claws on a rough wooden table, the priestess can see what ordinary mortals cannot. She gently throws the claws on the table and "reads" their positions to discern the whereabouts of Davy Jones and his crew.

Delicate pattern accentuates her hypnotic eyes

MAGIC NECKLACE
From a silver chain round Tia Dalma's neck hangs a curious pendant. Though the crab-shaped pendant is tarnished and has dulled with age, a mysterious face is still visible.

Chain made from the purest of silver

Crab claws

Dried plants are ground down to make potions

Jar holds locks of sirens' hair

Preserved sea snake

Swamp toad spawn used to heal many ailments

Vials filled with spider venom

On Land—Even at Sea

Tia Dalma tells Jack what he wants to know: where to find the *Flying Dutchman* and its captain, Davy Jones. To protect him from Davy's power, she gives Jack a jar of dirt, so that he'll always be near land—and safety.

A SIGHT FOR SORE EYES

Tia's shack is teeming with jars of weird objects and one in particular has Ragetti transfixed. In an iron-bound jar hanging from a rafter, float dozens of staring eyeballs. For most this grisly sight would be sickening but for Ragetti the eyeballs are beautiful to behold. For as long as he can remember, he has longed to exchange his wooden eye for the real thing and maybe now his dream will come true.

STRANGE ATTRACTION

Will's boyish good looks charm Tia Dalma. As soon as he enters the shack, she beams an inviting smile at him. Jack flatters himself that the grin is for him, and is shocked when his old sweetheart ignores him. She touches Will's face with her hand. "You have a touch of destiny in you, William Turner..." she tells him: though they have never met before, she knows his name.

Souls for Sale

In a terrifying bargain with Davy Jones, Jack Sparrow has just three days to find 100 human souls. If he succeeds, he will be a free man once more. If he fails, he faces a life of slavery, serving Jones on the *Flying Dutchman*. Fortunately, Jack knows just the place to look for souls—at the *Faithful Bride* tavern on the island of Tortuga, life is cheap. With help from Gibbs, Jack figures he can easily find enough desperate men to fulfill his side of the bargain. He might even do it before time runs out.

Lining up to Sell their Souls

The misfits who line up in the tavern have no idea of the fate Jack has in mind for them. Each man is blighted with an ailment—some are old and practically blind, a few are lame, and many have never set foot upon a ship in their lives. "What makes you think you're worthy to crew on the *Black Pearl*?" Gibbs asks them one by one. Their answers are pathetic, but Gibbs does not care. Anyone will do—as long as they have a soul to sell, and can sign on the dotted line.

Table in the tavern becomes Gibbs' desk

Pile of recruiting papers

Surprise Recruit

When James Norrington joins the line, Gibbs does not recognize him at first. Disgraced and no longer a commodore, he claims that he is determined to go back to sea and is even willing to join the pirates he once hunted. But old habits die hard, and Norrington pulls out a gun and takes aim at Jack.

SHARING A STY

Norrington's foolishness with the gun causes chaos. Drunken pirates love to fight, and here at last is the perfect excuse for a brawl. Norrington is on the losing side and ends up in the gutter with the pigs.

NORRINGTON AND MERCER

Elizabeth leaves Norrington alone on the docks where he is approached by Beckett's clerk, Mercer. In the shadows Mercer strikes a deal with the disgraced former commodore on behalf of his master.

THE BROKEN COMPASS

Just as the *Black Pearl* is about to sail, Jack gets another surprise recruit. It's Elizabeth, cunningly disguised as a sailor boy. Jack lies about how he betrayed Will—then realizes that Elizabeth's desire to rescue her fiancé will lead him to the chest. He tells her that the only way to save Will is to find the Dead Man's Chest that contains the heart of Davy Jones, knowing that her greatest wish will be to locate the chest. He hands her his compass and, as he predicted, the needle swings and holds steady in one direction, giving them their heading.

Davy Jones

Imagine a creature half human, half sea beast, with black eyes as soulless as a shark's, a claw for an arm, and a beard made of octopus tentacles. This nightmarish creature is Davy Jones, legendary ruler of the ocean depths. Doomed to cruise the oceans forever in his ghost-ship the *Flying Dutchman*, Jones offers drowning mariners the chance to live by joining his crew—a fate that turns out to be worse than death.

Heartless Beast

According to legend, Davy Jones fell in love with a woman "as harsh and untameable as the sea." He never stopped loving her and the pain it caused him was too much for him to bear so he carved out his heart and locked it away in a chest. He keeps the key to the chest with him at all times and the location of the chest is a closely guarded secret.

"BOOTSTRAP BILL"
Will Turner's father, "Bootstrap Bill," traded his soul with Davy Jones. A relatively new member of the *Flying Dutchman*'s crew, he remains more human than sea creature.

Stem is made from silver mined below the seabed

PIPING HOT
Carved from whalebone, Davy's pipe is rarely out of his mouth. He fills it with a mysterious mixture that burns so fiercely that it stays alight even in the deepest ocean.

Poor Wyvern!

The longer that
the mariners sail on the
Flying Dutchman, the worse
is their fate, for they slowly
become part of the ship. Wyvern
is almost as wooden as the ship's
beams and knuckles. There's still a bit
of human left in him, though, and he helps
Will find the key to the Dead Man's Chest.

Wyvern is barely able to break free

Wyvern's outstretched arm grips a ship's lantern

Father and Son

Reunited with his son on the
deck of the *Flying Dutchman*,
"Bootstrap Bill" only recognizes
Will as he's about to get a
lashing. He is determined to
help his son to escape from
Jones' clutches.

The key to the chest has a unique double-stem design

THE KEY TO JONES' HEART

Will shows Bootstrap the outline of the
key that Jack obtained in the Turkish prison.
Then, in a dangerous game of Liar's Dice, they
learn that Jones keeps it on a lanyard around his neck.
While Bootstrap stands watch, his son sneaks in to Jones'
cabin, and snatches the key from the sleeping captain.

Decorated with carvings of sea snakes

Wyvern is covered in coral and barnacles and is almost indistinguishable from the ship's hull

DEAD MAN'S CHEST

Davy Jones' heart still
beats inside the Dead Man's
Chest. Will learns that if he
can find the chest, open it, and
stab the beating heart, Davy
Jones will die. The doomed
crewmen of the *Flying
Dutchman* will at last be
released from their
fiendish bargain.

Elaborate lock resembles both a heart and a crab

The Flying Dutchman

When mariners awake screaming, it's because they have dreamed of a ghostly ship and its terrifying barnacled crew. In sailors' legends the *Flying Dutchman* rises from the ocean depths, its rigging draped in seaweed and its sails glowing like fire. It speeds across the flat water when all other ships are becalmed. Its very beams sigh with human voices, weighed down with a century of weary toil. When sailors fall overboard and are doomed to drown they soon realize that the *Dutchman* is not just a myth; the ship appears before their eyes and they are swiftly plucked from the jaws of death and given the option to serve before the mast of Davy Jones' ship.

Melancholy Music

Every evening haunting music envelops the ship. It comes from Davy Jones' vast pipe organ that appears to have grown like coral from the deck. The captain sits at the keyboard for hours at a time pouring all his sorrow into his mournful melodies. Above the keyboard is a carving of a woman with long flowing hair and surrounded by sea creatures. As he plays he seems to be tormented by the carving, clearly transfixed by the woman yet barely able look at her.

THE CANNON'S MOUTH
Every part of the *Dutchman* seems to be alive. Even the gunports grimace with human faces. When the ship goes on the attack, the row of mouths that line the hull open wide to show the bronze cannons within.

GRIM FIGUREHEAD

At the bows of the ghost-ship hangs a carved statue of the grim reaper. This legendary figure cuts off lives as if cutting corn with his scythe. It's a fitting figurehead. For Jones no longer simply collects the souls of drowning sailors. Now he drags them to their doom.

CAPTAIN'S CABIN

At the heart of the ship, Jones' cabin shimmers with the light of a million glowing deep-sea creatures. Its ornate panels are carved from the wrecks of sunken ships.

LAMPS ASTERN

Few human sailors ever see the stern of the *Flying Dutchman*—or if they do, it's the last thing they see. The pattern of windows in the ship's great cabin glow like the teeth of a grinning mouth. The deck above is decorated with the intertwined skeletons of ferocious sea beasts.

Isla Cruces

In the hands of Elizabeth, Jack's compass leads them to *Isla Cruces*. As the *Black Pearl* approaches the deserted island, Jack senses that he is just moments away from finding the Dead Man's Chest and being free of the terrible debt he owes Davy Jones. But unbeknown to Jack there are others who have set their sights on the chest...

Buried Treasure

Elizabeth leads them to the spot where the chest lies and they start to dig. Suddenly, a spade makes a hollow thud and Jack brushes away the sand to reveal a large chest. He pulls it out and hastily breaks the lock with the shovel.

BEACH FRONT BATTLE

At last Jack has what he wants and can use the heart to make Jones call off the Kraken but Will appears with the key and wants to stab the heart to release his father from slavery on board the *Flying Dutchman*. When Norrington also stakes his claim on the heart in order to regain his honor, a battle for the key ensues.

MISSING A BEAT

From the chest Jack pulls out mementoes of Jones' past love. Finally they hear the heart beating within a smaller chest.

Nautical Nasties

Jack, Norrington, and Will are busy fighting, unaware that the *Flying Dutchman* is looming ominously just offshore. Davy Jones cannot set foot upon land so he sends his ferocious crewmen to retrieve his heart. They emerge menacingly from the crystal-clear waters and make their way up the shore.

A Terrible Temptation

Having seen the *Dutchman* appear, Pintel and Ragetti flee for their lives only to find the others fighting. Realizing that everyone else is distracted they can't resist the opportunity to steal the precious chest and make their escape into the dense jungle, carrying it between them.

MAKING AN ESCAPE
Pintel and Ragetti's good fortune is short-lived and they soon regret taking the chest. Nothing could prepare them for their encounter with Jones' barnacle-encrusted army.

BALANCING ACT
When Jack, Will, and Norrington find themselves in an old mill, their battle takes on an unexpected twist. Will and Norrington end up balancing upon a huge mill wheel which breaks loose and hurtles through the jungle.

Journey's End

After a tireless fight with Will, Jack, and the crew of the *Flying Dutchman*, Norrington arrives filthy and bedraggled in Beckett's office. After a battle with so many twists and turns, who eventually won the heart? If Norrington can produce it he'll redeem himself and regain his place in society. But perhaps the heart is with Jack on the *Black Pearl* or even back with its owner, Davy Jones...

The Kraken

The Kraken is Davy Jones' obedient leviathan, sent to prey on unwary ships and mariners. With a hideous roar and a towering wave of foam and spray, a gigantic tentacle breaks the surface of the sea. Cold, clammy, slimy, and immensely strong, it wraps itself around the deck of a boat and crushes it like a matchstick. Then the head of the sea monster slowly rises from the waves. On its breath the terrified ship's crew smells the rotting corpses of a thousand drowned sailors. Its rolling eyes briefly focus, then it dives, dragging the doomed ship down to Davy Jones' Locker. The Kraken has struck again!

The Kraken wraps its tentacles around the ship before it pulls it down into the sea

The thick mast snaps in half like a twig

Tentacles slam into the deck, smashing the entire ship to splinters

Even in calm waters the Kraken causes the sea to churn and swirl as it rises from the depths

The beast uses the tips of its tentacles to feel its way around a ship before deciding where to strike next

The huge suckers on the Kraken's tentacles are strong enough to pull the flesh clean away from a sailor's face

SEA MONSTER

For centuries this beast of the deep has inspired fear among sailors. Few have seen the Kraken and lived to tell the tale. The monster is said to be the length of 10 ships, with immensely strong tentacles and a huge gaping mouth filled with rows of razor-sharp teeth.

Index

LONDON, NEW YORK, MUNICH,
MELBOURNE, AND DELHI

Senior Editor Lindsay Kent **Project Designer** Lisa Crowe
Publishing Manager Simon Beecroft **Designer** Cathy Tincknell
Category Publisher Alex Allan **Brand Manager** Lisa Lanzarini
Production Rochelle Talary **DTP Design** Lauren Egan & Hanna Ländin

First American edition, 2006
06 07 08 09 10 10 9 8 7 6 5 4 3 2 1
Published in the United States by DK Publishing, Inc.
375 Hudson Street, New York, New York 10014

ISBN-13: 978-0-75662-064-6
ISBN-10: 0-7566-2064-3

Reproduced by Media Development and Printing Ltd., UK
Leo Paper Products Ltd., China

Acknowledgments

The publisher would like to thank the following for their kind permission to reproduce their illustrations:

(key: a-above; c-centre; b-below; l-left; r-right; t-top)

Richard Bonson 28–31; Mauro Borelli 3r, 64–65 main illustration, 64t, 65t, 65c, 65b;
James Carson 52–53, 63l; Diane Chadwick 46–47; Crash McCreery 62, 64bl, 69br;
Robert Nelmes 8–9, 62–63; Nathan Schroeder 56–57.

The Publisher would also like to thank the following people:
Jerry Bruckheimer for kindly writing the foreword; Mary Mullen, Jon Rogers, Rich Thomas, Graham Barnard,
and Lisa Gerstel at Disney for all their help; Rick Heinrichs, Carla Nemec, Sarah Contant, and Megan Romero
at Second Mate Producions for their hospitality and invaluable advice.

Discover more at
www.dk.com